Mini-Mysteries Featuring

**The Mystery of
the Missing Teddy Bear**

**The Case of
the Lost Lasagna**

By Jim Kraft

Illustrated by Paws, Inc.

A GOLDEN BOOK • NEW YORK
Western Publishing Company, Inc., Racine, Wisconsin 53404

THE MYSTERY OF THE MISSING TEDDY BEAR

Garfield woke up at his usual time...just in time for lunch! "That certainly was a great night's sleep," he said. "I hope you slept well, Pooky." Garfield reached out to give his teddy bear a hug.

But there was no Pooky to hug!

"Pooky? Pooky, where are you?" asked Garfield. "That's funny. He was here when I got up for my midnight snack."

Garfield shook out his blanket. He checked under his bed. Pooky wasn't there.

"Pooky! Poooooky!" called Garfield as he ran through the house.
Garfield searched behind the TV.
He checked the laundry basket.

He even looked in the mailbox.
But he couldn't find Pooky anywhere! It could mean only
one thing—Pooky had been bearnapped.

"Some watchdog you are!" Garfield said to Odie. "You let someone come in and bearnap my Pooky! They'll probably want a ransom of a million dollars, and all I have in my piggy bank is two vanilla wafers!"

"Arf!" said Odie, who, as usual, didn't understand what was happening.

Then Garfield spied some chocolate crumbs around his bed. "Aha!" he cried. "This could be a clue. The bearnapper was eating something chocolate."

Garfield and Odie followed the trail of crumbs into the kitchen.

"Here's another clue!" cried Garfield. "The bearnapper drank some milk, too! He left a big print on this empty glass! Whoever he was, this bearnapper was hungry.

"Let's look at the facts," said Garfield. "We know that Pooky was taken sometime after midnight by a bearnapper who drank milk and ate chocolate." Suddenly Garfield smiled. "I've got it, Odie!" he shouted. "I know where Pooky is!"

Garfield raced across the kitchen to a cake plate sitting on the table. He lifted the cover...and there was Pooky!

"I had a glass of milk and a big piece of chocolate cake for my midnight snack," explained Garfield. "After that I was so sleepy that I left Pooky on the cake plate. I'm the bearnapper!"

Garfield was very glad that he had solved the mystery of the missing teddy bear. But he still had one question.

"Pooky, what happened to the last piece of cake? I know there was a piece left. And I know *you* didn't eat it. Teddy bears can't eat cake, right?"

Pooky couldn't answer, of course. He just sat there, looking stuffed.

THE CASE OF THE
LOST LASAGNA

"Great news, Garfield!" Jon Arbuckle announced. "I've been asked to judge the lasagna contest at the food fair today!"

"Why you?" asked Garfield. "*I'm* the lasagna expert around here."

"It's a competition between chefs from the three best Italian restaurants in town," Jon continued. "Would you like to come along?"

Garfield grabbed a knife and fork. "I'm ready when you are!" he said.

When Garfield and Jon arrived, the three chefs were
already hard at work. Chef Ravioli, Chef Spaghettini, and
Chef Macaroni quickly turned bowls of meat, cheese, noodles,
and sauce into three pans of lasagna. Then they popped the
pans into three separate ovens.

Soon a wonderful aroma filled the air, making Garfield's
mouth water.

Finally, when Garfield thought he couldn't wait any longer, the oven timers rang. Chef Ravioli and Chef Spaghettini each took a pan of steaming lasagna from the oven.

But Chef Macaroni suddenly cried out, "Somebody stole my lasagna!" He held up his pan. Except for a few drips of sauce, it was empty!

"GARFIELD!" cried Jon

"I'm innocent, I swear!" claimed Garfield. "I never even nibbled a noodle!"

"I knew I shouldn't trust you around lasagna," said Jon. "Now you've ruined the whole contest!"

Chef Macaroni was very upset. "This is an outrage!" he shouted. "Someone should call the police!"

"I'll show Jon," vowed Garfield. "I'll catch the crook who stole that lasagna. But first I'd better taste the evidence."

He dipped a finger into the sauce left in Chef Macaroni's pan. "Hmm," thought Garfield. "This sauce is cold, and so is the pan."

Garfield opened the door to Chef Macaroni's oven. "This oven should still be hot, but it's not," observed Garfield.

Then he recalled something else peculiar. "A chef always wears a chef's cap," thought Garfield. "What happened to Chef Macaroni's cap?"

Garfield knew he had to find that chef's cap. He looked all around the kitchen. Finally his nose led him to a cupboard above Chef Macaroni's stove.

In the meantime, Chef Macaroni was arguing with Jon. "My lasagna would have been the best!" he exclaimed. "I think I deserve First Prize anyway!"

While the chef argued, Garfield sneaked up behind him. "I believe you lost this," said Garfield.

Garfield slapped the chef's cap on Chef Macaroni's head. Instantly meat, cheese, noodles, and sauce poured down over the chef's face.

"What's going on here?" demanded Jon.

"All right, all right, I confess," sputtered Chef Macaroni. "I stole my own lasagna! You see, I forgot to turn my oven on! I was too embarrased to enter a pan of unbaked lasagna, so I quickly dumped the lasagna into my cap and threw it into the cupboard. I fooled everyone, except Garfield."

"Never match wits with a cat," said Garfield.

"I'm sorry, Garfield," said Jon. "I shouldn't have accused you. Can you ever forgive me?"

"Not in a hundred million years," grumbled Garfield.

"I brought you some lasagna," said Jon. "Now will you forgive me?"

Garfield stuffed the lasagna into his mouth. Then he smiled and said, "I'll let you know after you bring me dessert!"